Christopher-

HENRY

JAMES

Hugs + kisses-
Gramma +
Grampa

PERCY

TITLES AVAILABLE IN BUZZ BOOKS

First published 1990 by Buzz Books,
an imprint of the Octopus Publishing Group,
Michelin House, 81 Fulham Road, London SW3 6RB

LONDON   MELBOURNE   AUCKLAND

Copyright © William Heinemann Ltd 1990

All publishing rights: William Heinemann Ltd. All television
and merchandising rights licensed by William Heinemann Ltd
to Britt Allcroft (Thomas) Ltd exclusively, worldwide.

Photographs © Britt Allcroft (Thomas) Ltd 1985
Photographs by David Mitton and Kenny McArthur
for Britt Allcroft's production of Thomas the
Tank Engine and Friends.

ISBN 1 85591 029 2

Printed and bound in the UK by BPCC Paulton Books Ltd

THOMAS'S CHRISTMAS PARTY

buzz books

It was Christmas on the Island of Sodor. All the engines were working hard. Thomas and Toby were busy carrying people and parcels up and down the branch line. Everyone was happy.

Only the coaches, Annie and Clarabel, were complaining.

"It's always the same before Christmas," they groaned. "We feel so full, we feel so full."

"Oh, come on," said Thomas as he puffed out of the station. "Where's your festive spirit?"

"Leave that to the others. All we get is hard work," said the coaches.

"Cheer up," said Thomas. "Christmas Day is almost here."

By the side of the track was a lonely little cottage with a familiar figure standing by the gate, waving to them.

"It's Mrs Kyndley," whistled Thomas. "Peep! Peep! Happy Christmas!"

However heavy the loads, Thomas always felt better for seeing Mrs Kyndley.

"Christmas just wouldn't be Christmas without Mrs Kyndley," he said and puffed thoughtfully on.

When work was over Thomas went to see the other engines. It was a scene of great celebration. Their coats had been polished and they felt very proud of themselves.

"Huh," said Gordon. "Just look at us —
your driver will have to work fast to get you
to look as smart as us."

"Never mind that," replied Thomas.
"I've something important to say. Do you
realise it's a whole year since Mrs Kyndley
saved us from a nasty accident? You
remember when she was ill in bed and . . ."

"Yes, of course," interrupted Edward. "You told us how she waved her red dressing gown out of her window to warn you about a landslide on the line ahead."

"And you and Toby gave her presents," Percy joined in, "and the Fat Controller sent her to Bournemouth to get better."

"But," said James and Henry together, "the rest of us never really thanked her properly."

16

"Exactly," said Thomas, triumphantly.
"So now I think we should all give her a
special Christmas party."

The big engines were delighted, and so were their drivers and firemen.

"We'd like that," they said. "A party will be fun. We'll ask the Fat Controller."

The drivers felt sure that the
Fat Controller would agree as, indeed, he
did.

"A party for Mrs Kyndley?" said the
Fat Controller. "What a splendid idea,
Thomas. Mrs Kyndley is a very good friend
to us all."

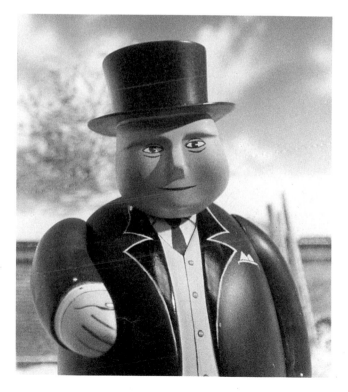

Everyone was looking forward to the party, and the engines were soon making plans. Then, suddenly, silence fell. The Fat Controller had bad news.

"The weather's changed," he said.
"Mrs Kyndley is all snowed up – Toby says
he will help to rescue her. You must help
too, Thomas – there's no party unless you
do!"

21

Thomas hated snow but he said bravely, "I'll try, sir. We must rescue her, we must."

"There's a good engine," smiled the Fat Controller. "You and Toby will manage splendidly."

The men came to fit Thomas with a snow plough.

Thomas and Toby set off to the rescue. Thomas charged the snowdrifts fiercely. Sometimes he swept them aside, sometimes they stuck fast.

When they stuck, Thomas and Toby drew back so that men from the van could loosen the hard-packed snow. Then on they went again.

It was hard and tiring work for everybody. But when they came to the cutting near the cottage they could go no further.

"Look at that!" exclaimed Thomas's fireman.

"Peep, peep, peep! Here we are!" whistled Thomas.

The snow was so deep round the house
that the answering wave had to come from
an upstairs window.

"Toot, toot, tooooot! So are we!" came a
voice from behind the cottage.

"That's Terence!" said Thomas excitedly.
"He's come to help, too."

Sure enough, Terence had a snow plough
and was working hard to clear a path to the
railway line and safety.

At long last the rescue was complete. Percy arrived to take the tired workmen home. Terence said goodbye to Mrs Kyndley, and promised to take care of her cottage as he watched them all set off.

The engines made good time. No more snow had fallen but the yard was dark when they arrived at Tidmouth. The shed doors were shut, there was silence and there was no one to be seen.

Thomas's heart sank.

Then suddenly all the lights went on. What a marvellous sight awaited Mrs Kyndley!

"Well done," said the Fat Controller, smiling happily. "I'm really proud of you all."

Mrs Kyndley especially thanked the smaller engines.

"Thomas and Toby are old friends," she said, "and now, Percy, you are my friend too."

Percy was so pleased that he bubbled over.

"Three cheers for Mrs Kyndley," he cried.

"Peep, peep, peep!" they all whistled.

The Fat Controller held his ears but everyone else laughed and joined in.

"Right, everyone," he said. "One, two, three . . ."

"HAPPY CHRISTMAS, MRS KYNDLEY!"

All the engines whistled and everyone began to sing:

28

We wish you a Merry Christmas!
We wish you a Merry Christmas!
We wish you a Merry Christmas
And a Happy New Year!

Thomas the Tank Engine and his friends thought it was the best Christmas ever and Mrs Kyndley could think of nowhere she would rather live than here, with them, on the Island of Sodor.

THOMAS

EDWARD

GORDON